OFF-the-GRID KID

Written by
Bronwyn Preece

Illustrated by
Karla Lironi

Eifrig Publishing LLC
Berlin Lemont

Your Personalized Book!

CREATOR: Make your own personal audio recording of this book. Simply download the free StorySticker app on your Apple or Android mobile device, or visit www.storysticker.com. Scan the image or enter the 10-letter code to begin. Once you have set up an account and logged in, you can start to record yourself reading the story one page at a time. Once you have created your own special personalized storytime, you can share it with the recipient of your book!

RECIPIENT: Just follow the instructions on the app or website to listen to the recording created just for you.

TQLXHZTBQP

Published by Eifrig Publishing,
PO Box 66, Lemont, PA 16851, USA
Knobelsdorffstr. 44, 14059 Berlin, Germany.

For information regarding permission, write to:
Rights and Permissions Department,
Eifrig Publishing,
PO Box 66, Lemont, PA 16851, USA.
permissions@eifrigpublishing.com, +1-888-340-6543

Library of Congress Cataloging-in-Publication Data
Preece, Bronwyn
Off-the-Grid Kid
by Bronwyn Preece, illustrated by Karla Lironi
p. cm.

Paperback: ISBN 978-1-63233-285-1
Hardcover: ISBN 978-1-63233-309-4
Ebook: ISBN 978-1-63233-137-3

[1. Environment - Juvenile Non-fiction.]
I. Lironi, Karla, ill. II. Title: Off-the-Grid Kid

25 24 23 22 2021
5 4 3 2
Printed on acid-free recycled paper. ∞

4

I live in a cabin by the sea,
powered by a windmill up on top of a tree,
solar panels that gather energy from the sun,
and a waterwheel that spins
in the stream that runs.

I live in a cabin by the sea,
on the small and beautiful island of Lasqueti.
In the middle of the Georgia Strait,
on this off-the-grid isle our home we make.

Off-the-Grid is so defined ...
by no power poles or electrical lines.
There are no transformers, no overhead towers.

Here, the burning of coal does not play a role,
neither do dams, nor the Tar Sands.
Plus, nuclear reactors are never a factor.

Instead,
we tread
more lightly on the land.

We create and generate
our own power by means
that are considered green.

I live in a cabin by the sea,
where we collect our water in tanks
high atop the hill,
gathering rain, when passing clouds spill.
It then courses through pipes
for our cups, sink,
and my bath to fill.

I live in a cabin by the sea,
where we chop wood for the stove
that heats our home.
With a small hatchet,
I split the kindling . . .
but never alone!

11

I live in a cabin by the sea,
where we grow and gather most of the food that we eat,
a diet always filled with wild and wholesome organic treats.

I live in a cabin by the sea,
where when you need to pee or do number two,
you go outside to the outhouse – or, as we call it,
The Lovely Loo – designed in such a way
that it then composts the poo.

15

I live in a cabin by the sea,
in a home that is never locked
and has no key.

I live in a cabin by the sea,
where my Mom, my Dad and me
(which makes three!)
all live very comfortably!

We live in a vibrant island community,
of just over 300 folk.
Some people live on the water in anchored boats,
some in homes nestled into nooks in the woods,
or wee cottages cradled in coves.
    Others live in open fields,
      or perched on the edge of a rocky ledge,
      or sheltered in a cozy abode
      tucked away at the end of the road.

We *live in a vibrant island community*,
that is reached by passenger-only ferry.
There are cars, trucks,
and other-wheeled things,
but they've all come by barge,
so they are few and far between.

We live in a vibrant island community,
where people pull together cooperatively:
helping neighbors, friends and family,
building the new barn for the farm,
weeding the garden now overgrown,
and feeding the next-door chickens
on the days not home.

Carpooling to events lessens
our carbon footprint dents.

23

We *live in a vibrant island community*,
with a school, a bakery, a restaurant and store,
veggie stands, a daycare, a market and more.
The very best place to visit is our Free Store:
with price-tag free "shopping" galore!

We have a Hall where we gather to dance,
play music, create art, host festivals and fairs,
buy, sell, and trade homemade wares.

We live in a vibrant island community,
surrounded by big, towering trees,
springs from which water bubbles and teems,
alongside bursting gardens
that have been grown from saved seeds.

Steeped in forests
bordered by shores
of oysters and clams,
the people living here
live *with* the land.

We live in a vibrant island community,
surrounded by a world
being devastated environmentally.
Wars over oil and rigs imploding,
deforestation, over-fishing
and species rapidly disappearing.

Smoke plumes, toxic fumes, pesticides and waste,
pollution, destruction, all happening
at such a quickening pace.

**We ALL live in a world being devastated
environmentally,
where now our every action must be measured
accordingly.**

And yet, and so, and still...
Together we can live
collectively and cooperatively
with every being – animals, people, and places,
taking care and leaving little or no traces . . .

Which is why . . .

I live in a cabin by the sea,
as part of a vibrant island community,
where my Mom, my Dad, and me
(which makes three!)
are trying our very best to live responsibly!

Bronwyn Preece lives by the sea on Lasqueti — an honored guest on the Traditional Territory of the Straits Salish People — with her daughter, partner, three horses, and cat! As an improvisational performance eARThist and writer, she marries her passion for artistic expression with activism. She performs and facilitates workshops internationally. Currently pursuing a PhD, she holds an MA and BFA in Applied Theater and is the pioneer of earthBODYment. Her other books include *Gulf Islands Alphabet* (2012) and *In the Spirit of Homebirth* (2015).

She served two terms in local politics, being the youngest woman ever elected to her post with the Islands Trust, the municipal-level government for the Gulf Islands of British Columbia. Bronwyn can often be found out on long walks, fermenting batches of sauerkraut and kombucha, or shamelessly hugging trees.

Please visit: www.bronwynpreece.com

Karla Lironi was born on Lasqueti Island and has lived there for much of her life. She has a one-room cabin, which she shares with her cat and baby grand piano! She enjoys sailing and gardening. Karla participates in the artistic life of the community through both visual and the performing arts. You can find her poems in *Paper Birds* (2010).

Karla is a graduate of the visual arts program at Camosun College. Her paintings are full of color and light and have a whimsical quality that lifts the heart.

CPSIA information can be obtained
at www.ICGtesting.com
Printed in the USA
LVHW070123230321
682196LV00019B/287

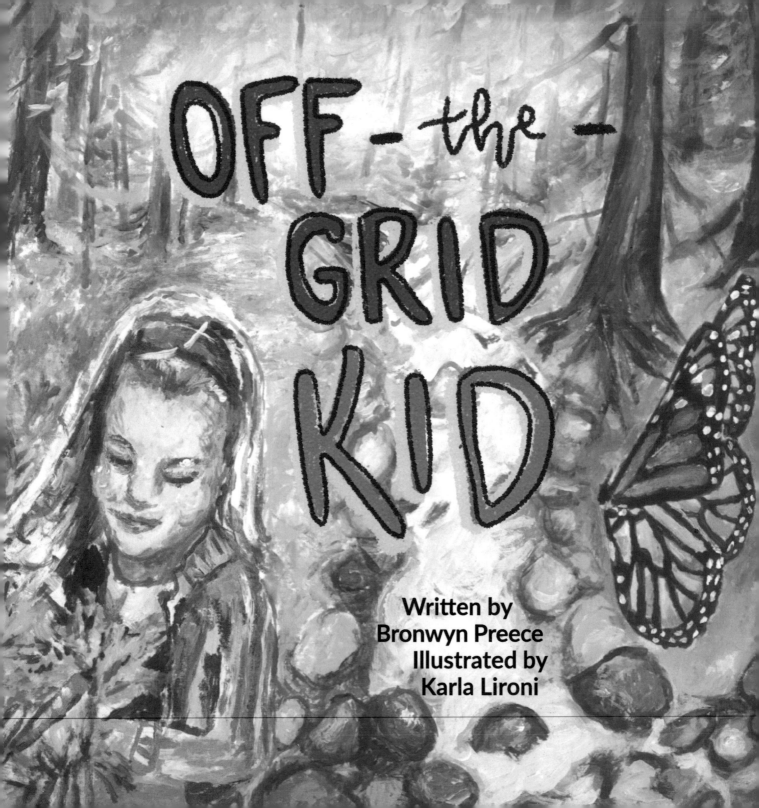

OFF - the - GRID KID

Written by
Bronwyn Preece
Illustrated by
Karla Lironi